For my wife Ginny, my partner in
all things donuts and dancing

Special thanks to Katie Weaver
for an incredible cover design

Younger Media, LLC
www.YoungerMeAcademy.com

Author: Ben Okon
Illustrator: Komal Sharma

Dinos Love Donuts

Library of Congress Control Number: 2024913549
ISBN: 978-1-961428-20-1 (Paperback)

Younger Media, LLC offers special discounts when purchasing in higher quantities. For more information, please visit our website: www.YoungerMeAcademy.com

Published in USA (Birmingham, AL)

DINOS Love DONUTS

Ben Okon

Komal Sharma

DINOS do love donuts!
Did you know that in your KNOW-nut?
You might think my mind has BLOWN but
you should watch these DINOS GO-nuts!

They dip donuts deep in
JELLY,

stack some
SPRINKLES
on their bellies,

Why are they OBSESSED, you say?

'cause holey food is good for prey!
It helps see danger far away
while dishing up sweet dough all day.

But that's not ALL that **DINOS** like!
The holes fit great on horns and spikes!

For those with arms like LITTLE TIKES
a stick can reach, no need to pike!

These **DINOS** do love ONE thing more than donuts, if I might.
They love to **DANCE** from dawn to dusk and all throughout the night!

TRICERATOPS try TANGO
since the TRI-STEP is too TRITE,

"YEP! TANGO iS WAY BETTER!"

and the RAPTORS rep the
RHUMBA with a
RHYTHM razor-TIGHT.

Why do **DINOS** love to dance? Because they are so **BIG!**

The steps they take make palm trees **SHAKE** and **WIGGLE** with their jig.

Their footprints make great pools to SPLASH-

no need for them to DIG!

Their DANCES make the dust
float 'round their heads like WACKY WIGS!

The **DINOS'** big ol' bellies
mean they need to eat a LOT!

They'll wait in line all day at D's!
"Come get 'em while they're **HOT!**"

By the time it's time to dance, their jumbo tummies turn to knots! That's why the **BIGGEST** donuts are the ones that hit the spot!

You sure did
pay attention,
FRIEND,
you truly are
ALRIGHT!

The **DINOS** will all love it! Let's go dance all through the night!

FRIEND, I **HAVE** to ask you
ONE MORE THING before we roll:

Where **EXACTLY** did you hide
that **GIANT DONUT HOLE?!**

DINOS HATE the centers!
Yep, the OUTSIDES are their goal!

The centers look like rocks
(which scare the **DINOS** to their souls).

If a rock is on the dance floor
and it's stepped on. . .
it's a **SHOCK!**

And if a **DINO** eats one by mistake it might just **KNOCK**
that **DINO'S** teeth out of its mouth
until it screams out:

HOLY FIDDLESTICKS!

You brought the hole? Let that thing roll!
Let's push it **DOWN** this grassy knoll!

The **DINOS**—they must never know!
OK, we're hole-less, now let's go!

AHHHH! A rock! It's in the sky!

Let's RUN or we'll get hurt!

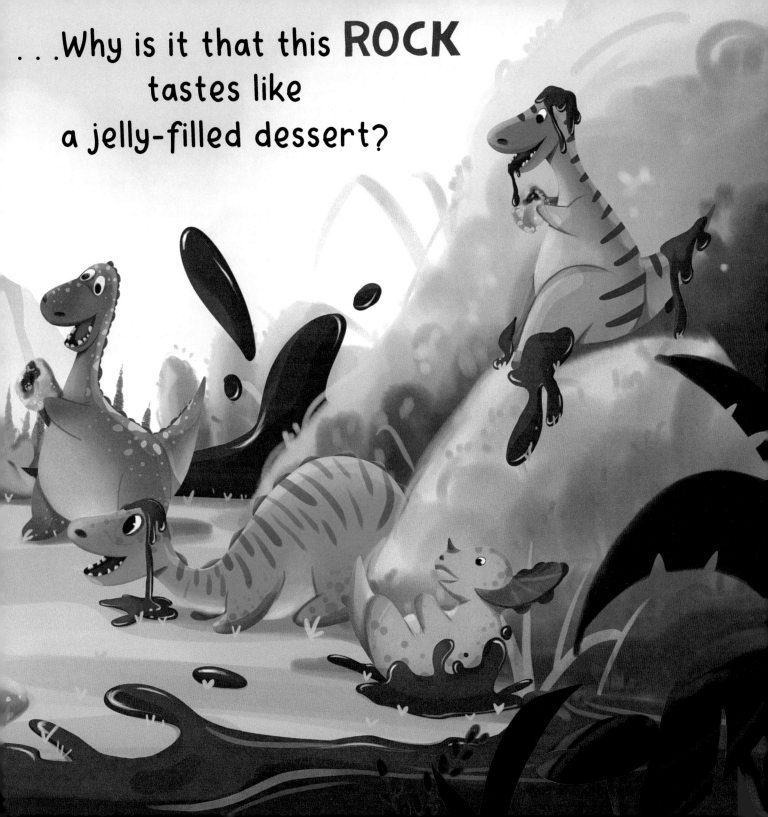

They're making all that noise for **YOU!**
A great big **DINO** cheer!

I bet they won't run scared the
next time big rocks are too near...

. . .and I'm
SURE
that you'll be
WELCOME
on their dance floor
EVERY
YEAR!

GET A RHYMING RECIPE FOR
DINO-MITE
ASTEROID BITES

"The Bite That Might Wipe You Out"

Scan here or go to
www.YoungerMeAcademy.com/dinoslovedonutscontent

Made in United States
Orlando, FL
30 September 2024

52135309R00024